MAX & MOLLY'S SPRING

Written and Illustrated
by
Ann Garrison Greenleaf

DERRYDALE BOOKS
New York • Avenel, New Jersey

FOR KATE, KATIE AND KATHLEEN—
WHO HELPED ME MAKE A MOUNTAIN OUT OF A MOLE HILL

This 1993 edition is published by Derrydale Books,
distributed by Outlet Book Company, Inc., a Random House Company,
40 Engelhard Avenue, Avenel, New Jersey 07001,
by arrangement with the author.

Random House
New York • Toronto • London • Sydney • Auckland

Printed and bound in the United States of America

ISBN 0-517-09153-4

10 9 8 7 6 5 4 3 2 1

One cloud and then another,

And the sky

is gray with showers;

One bud

and then another,

And the field

is full of flowers.

One twig

and then another,

And old nests

are snug again;

One task

and then another,

And spring cleaning

chores begin.

One peck

and then another,

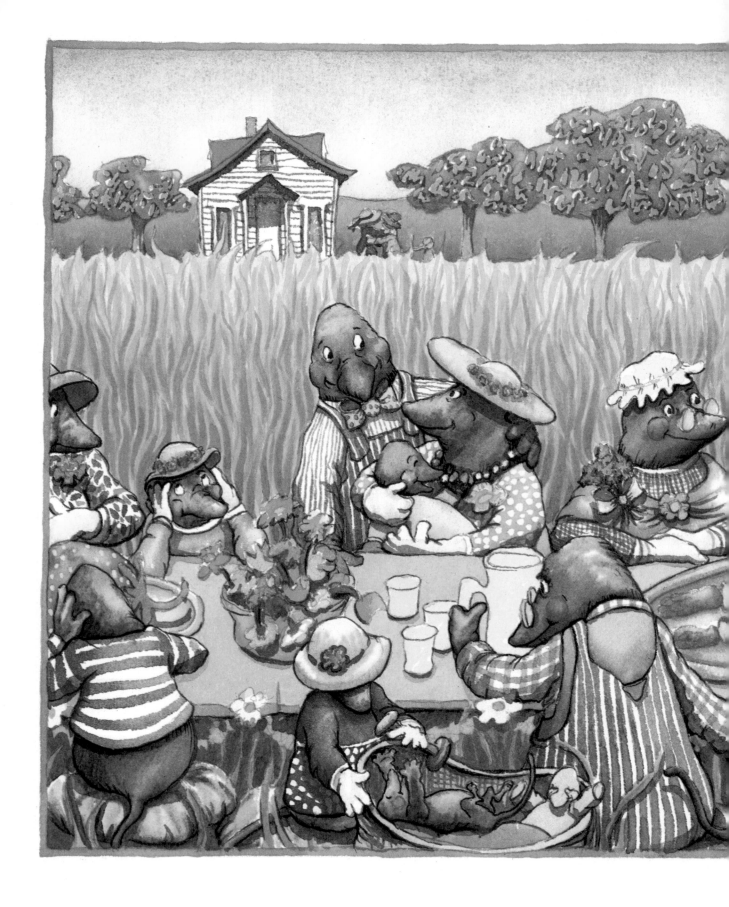

And the smallest chick

is hatched;

One stitch

and then another,

And the longest tear

is patched.

One row

and then another,

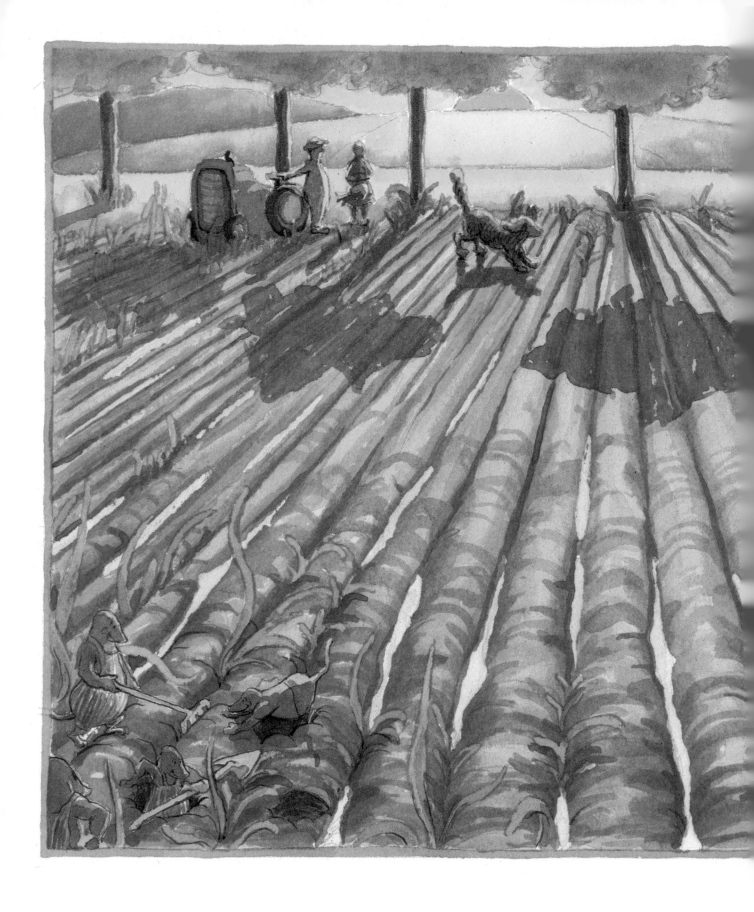

And the soil

is tilled and hoed;

One seed

and then another,

And a summer crop is sowed.